BLAST OFF BOY AND BLORP

FIRST DAY ON A STRANGE NEW PLANET

NEW PET

THE BIG SCIENCE FAIR

Blast Off Boy was chosen to go to school on planet Meep because he was so average. So were his grades! Now he's going to school with some of the greatest minds in the universe. Ugh! What's a regular guy to do on a planet of geniuses?

Blorp loves school on Earth. He actually looks forward to the challenge of pop quizzes, book reports, and, especially, science projects! He tried his best to convince his English teacher that he needed to bring in a real whale for his book report on *Moby Dick*.

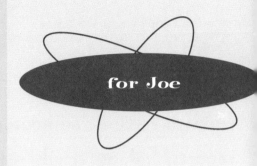

for Joe

Visit www.hyperionchildrensbooks.com
First Edition
1 3 5 7 9 10 8 6 4 2
Printed in Singapore

Library of Congress Cataloging-in-Publication Data on file.
ISBN 0-7868-0580-3 (trade)
ISBN 0-7868-1430-6 (pbk.)

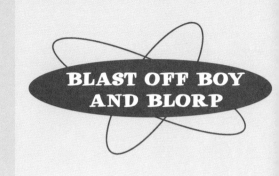

BLAST OFF BOY
AND BLORP

THE BIG
SCIENCE FAIR

written and illustrated by
DAN YACCARINO

Hyperion Paperbacks for Children
New York

"**I** have some exciting news,
class," Professor Plotz announced.
"Our school is going to have a big science fair,
and the best projects will get a prize!"

The class cheered. Well, everyone except Blast
Off Boy, that is. He didn't think science was at all
his best subject. But then, neither were advanced
nuclear calculus, quantum chemistry, or galactic
gym. And he wasn't too sure about recess, either.

"Oh, no," he groaned.

"What is it, Blast Off Boy?" asked Buzz.

"Aren't you excited about the big science fair?" asked Bo.

"Are you kidding?" Blast Off Boy whispered loudly. "Back on Earth, science was my worst subject! I've never been good at it! I'll never win! Ugh!"

"Blast Off Boy, this science fair is going to be fun! So stop worrying so much about winning or losing, and have a good time!" said Buzz.

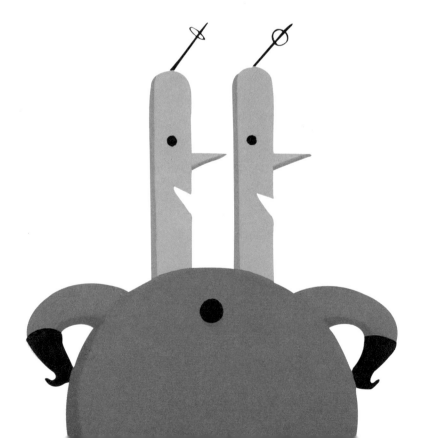

"Hey, you never know! Maybe you'll get a prize, after all!" said Bo. "Buzz and I are going to make a scale model of a helium molecule."

"No, we aren't," said Buzz. "We're going to make a diorama of the entire known universe, using toothpicks."

"Says who?" asked Bo.

"Says me," answered Buzz.

"I'm doomed," said Blast Off Boy.

On Earth, Lenny tried to keep up as Blorp raced home from school to tell his hosts, the Smiths, and their dog, Scooter, about the big science fair.

"There's a science fair at school," he excitedly told Mrs. Smith. "And I'm going to win first prize and get an award and have my picture in the newspaper and be on television and . . ."

"Now, calm down, Blorp," said Mrs. Smith. "Sit down and tell me all about it."

"I can't!" Blorp said excitedly. "I've got work to do!" So he raced upstairs to his room and let Lenny fill Mom in on the details.

For the rest of the day, Blorp stayed upstairs, planning out his brilliant, award-winning science project.

On planet Meep the next morning, the school yard was all abuzz about macaroni models of hydrogen molecules, homemade atom splitters, and dry-cell-battery-powered particle disrupters.

Blast Off Boy wished everyone would just change the subject already.

"Well, well, well, if it isn't Blast Off Boy. What are you going to do—" sarcastically asked Zax Zlobo, the smartest and, incidentally, the most obnoxious kid in school, "build a subatomic nose picker?"

"Don't you wish, Zlobo!" Blast Off Boy angrily replied.

This kid picked on Blast Off Boy every chance he got. Why didn't he just leave him alone? "My science project is a big secret, but let me tell you, it'll beat yours any day!" Blast Off Boy snapped.

A crowd started to gather and cheered when Blast Off Boy challenged Zax Zlobo.

"Wow!" said Buzz. "I didn't know you had even decided on what your project was."

"Yeah," said Bo, "let alone that it's gonna beat Zax Zlobo's!"

"You must have some great idea!" said Buzz.

"I must be crazy," said Blast Off Boy.

In homeroom, Blorp proudly announced to the whole class, "My science project will certainly be the biggest and best project at the fair, and, therefore, I will win first prize."

"Thank you, Blorp," said Ms. Jacobs. "I'm pleased that you are enthusiastic about the science fair." She reminded the children that the purpose of the science fair was to develop new ideas, experiment, and, most of all, to learn and have fun!

She asked the students to share their project ideas with the rest of the class.

Lucy Lumas loved science and wanted to be a scientist when she grew up. She said she planned to construct a model of an underwater city of the future. Arnie Tinkleman said he'd bring in his turtle, Chuck, but Ms. Jacobs reminded him that he had brought Chuck in last year and would have to think of something new this year. Sheldon Lutz had already forgotten there even was a science fair, but then he usually forgot his sneakers on gym day, too.

After school, Blorp, with the assistance of Lenny and Scooter, started to build his fabulous project.

"But, Blorp," said Lenny after Blorp had told him what the magificent machine would do, "there's a much easier way to do that. Let me show you."

Blorp waved him away, not wanting to hear anything but how wonderful his idea was. So Lenny kept quiet and just handed him tools.

Later, Mrs. Smith noticed that the blender had mysteriously disappeared, as well as some important pieces of the clothes dryer. Mr. Smith couldn't find his lawn mower, car jack, or treadmill. It seemed that every hour something new was discovered to be missing.

"**E**veryone at school is talking about your big, secret, prize-winning science fair project, Blast Off Boy!" Blippy said at dinner that evening.

"Is that so?" said Mr. Glorp. "Well, tell us all about it."

Blast Off Boy explained that if he talked about it, it wouldn't be secret anymore.

But, actually, he had no idea what to do, and he was starting to get worried. He was so busy thinking that everyone else's project would be far better than anything he could come up with, he didn't even bother to think of a project.

The only prize I'll ever get, he thought, will be last prize.

Well, on Earth, the big day finally arrived. Blorp and Lenny wheeled a huge contraption covered with Mrs. Smith's best sheets into the

gymnasium where the science fair was being held.
Everyone oohed and aahed at the sight of the
massive mysterious science project.

The judges, Principal Schultz and Ms. Jacobs, looked over all of the students' projects, including Arnie Tinkleman's new parakeet, also named

Chuck, who balanced toothpicks in its beak.
Sheldon Lutz brought his sneakers. He thought
it was gym day.

"Okay, Blorp," said Principal Schultz, "you may unveil your project now."

Lenny gave a drumroll.

"TA-DA!" cried Blorp as he pulled the sheet off what was certainly the biggest science project ever constructed for the annual science fair.

"Well, Blorp, what does it do?" asked Ms. Jacobs after examining the curious contraption.

"Let me show you," Blorp proudly said as he picked up a can of chili.

He placed it on one end of the machine, pulled a lever, and began cranking a handle while Scooter ran on a wheel.

The machine started to spin and whir. Toots, squeaks, and honks sounded off as the can of chili slowly turned around.

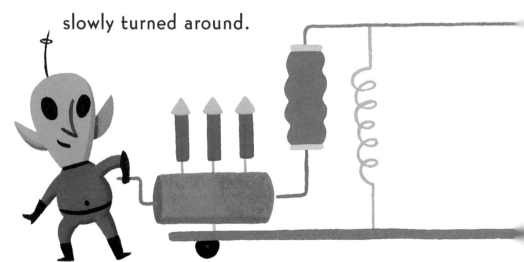

Then the machine stopped, and the noises ceased.

"You see," Blorp proudly exclaimed, "it opens cans! I call it a can opener! Isn't that brilliant?"

Ms. Jacobs quickly summoned someone from the lunchroom to bring a simple can opener.

"You mean it's been invented already?" Blorp asked in amazement. He thought he was the first to think of such an idea.

Lucy Lumas won first prize for her underwater city.

Blorp got an honorary prize for his effort and enthusiasm, rather than his practicality. While Scooter enjoyed the chili, Blorp apologized to Lenny for not listening to him and for being so caught up in his desire to win.

Then, Blorp turned around and discovered that the whole class was playing on his project—swinging, climbing, and crawling through it.

"Hmmm. This is just the thing the playground needs!" said Principal Schwartz.

Blorp felt as if he had won first prize!

On Meep, Blast Off Boy was upset. "Lunchtime is almost over, guys," sighed Blast Off Boy, "and I still don't have a project. I'm in big trouble."

Buzz and Bo tried their best, but all they could say was "We told you so, Blast Off Boy." For a week they had encouraged him to have fun, while all Blast Off Boy could do was complain about how there was no chance of his winning anything, so why try?

The bell rang. It was time for the judging.

Blast Off Boy, desperate, quickly hatched a plan.
He grabbed some Pluto beans from his uneaten
lunch, put them in a milk carton, smushed them
around, then "watered" them with Jupiter Cola.

"Maybe I'll get away with a D-minus," he said.

There his sad little science project sat, the last in a long line of particle hydrators, electron microscopes, and grape-juice-powered rockets, all constructed with scientific accuracy and superior intellect.

As Blast Off Boy's project sat alone in the sun-light, something happened. It started to sprout!

By the time the judges got to it, the strange plant was more than ten feet tall!

Professor Plotz asked Blast Off Boy to explain exactly what it was.

"I—I got some Pluto beans," he said, looking at his feet, "and watered them with Jupiter Cola."

Blast Off Boy was sure he was in big trouble now.

"Brilliant!" cried Professor Plotz.

"That's what this science fair is all about, young man! Experimentation!" He told the class that Blast Off Boy had taken two things we see every day and combined them in an unusual way.

Not only did Blast Off Boy's project win a prize for best experiment, it ate Zax Zlobo! Unfortunately, Principal Floont made it spit him out later.

"See?" said Buzz.

"Yeah, we told you it could be fun, Blast Off Boy!" said Bo. "Yeah! And you even got a prize!"

BLAST OFF BOY
AND BLORP

DON'T MISS
BLAST OFF BOY AND
BLORP'S ADVENTURES IN

First Day on a Strange New Planet

written and illustrated by
DAN YACCARINO

Hyperion Paperbacks for Children
New York

"Swell, the only free seat is next to a kid with two heads. Gross."

As the bus zoomed along, the other kids laughed and talked about their summer vacations floating in the Milky Way and touring the moons of Jupiter. Blast Off Boy stared out the window, watching the stars fly by.

"Hi! My name is Buzzopod," said one head.

"And my name is Bozopod," said the other.

"But you can call us Buzz and Bo," the two heads said together.

"Uh, hi," said Blast Off Boy, still looking out the window.

Blast Off Boy wished he was back in his old school, back on his old planet, good old Earth. He knew everybody there. The kids are weird and strange here, he thought. This stinks.

Meanwhile, back on good old Earth, Blorp could hardly contain himself. He had just met his new family, Mr. and Mrs. Smith, their son Lenny, and their dog, Scooter.

"I'm looking forward to my first day at Davis Elementary," he said. "You know, I've never been anywhere outside my solar system before!"

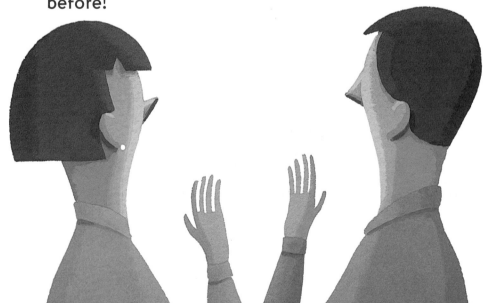

In homeroom, Blorp was so excited, he kept floating up to the ceiling.

"Please take your seat, Blorp," said Ms. Jacobs.

The other students quietly moved their desks away from him. Blorp didn't notice, and he wouldn't have cared anyway. He was in a new school on a new planet, and he was happy.

Dan Yaccarino is an award-winning artist and author, who has created many books for children, as well as the animated television series for children *Oswald*. He lives with his wife and children in New York City.

The inspiration for the Blast Off Boy and Blorp series came from Dan Yaccarino's experience of moving to a new home. Several nonerupting model volcanoes and pipe-cleaner atom molecule constructions earned him a solid C+ average in his third-favorite subject, science.